The Berenstain Bears' ®

PERFECT FISHING SPOT

Stan & Jan Berenstain

Reader's Digest **Kids**

Westport, Connecticut

Do you know
what I wish?
I wish that for dinner
we could have fish.

A fine fat fish,
tender and sweet.
There is nothing better
in the world to eat!

A fish would be fine.

But there's no need to fuss.

Just go and buy one

from Grizzly Gus.

May Sister and I
come with you, Dad?

Yes, indeed.
Of course, my lad.

But, Papa! Ma said go
to Grizzly Gus!

That's true, my son.
But just between us,
if you want a fish
that's tender and sweet,
a fish that's a wonderful treat
for a bear to eat—

Then dig up some worms,
get out your pole,

and head for your favorite
fishing hole.

Your fishing hole
looks small, Papa Bear.
Can there really be
a big fish in there?

Of course there can.

I've got one now!

Just watch your dad.

He'll show you how

to catch a fish

that's tender and sweet,

a fish that's a treat

for a bear to eat!

Papa, that fish
may be tender and sweet.
But it's much too small
for us to eat.

Hmm. The big ones have all
been caught, you see,
caught years ago
by guess who? ME!

I know a better
fishing spot!

I can taste that fish,
tender, hot,
a fish to do
our family proud...

I see, I see.

Good day to you!

Er…my cubs and I

were enjoying the view!

This fish, Dad,
will you catch it soon?
I think it must be
afternoon!

Don't bother me
with questions, please.
I know a spot
just past those trees!

Look, cubs! Look!
I've got a bite!
Whatever I've hooked,
just look at it fight!

Look how it thrashes!
Look how it sloshes!

Dad, that isn't a fish!
It's a pair of galoshes!

This way, cubs!
Follow me!
We will get our fish
from the deep blue sea!

BOATS
RENTED

Look at them all!

They'll sink our boat!

Throw 'em back!

We must stay afloat!

Help! Help!
Look, Papa Bear!
We're going up!
Up in the air!

Boat and all!
In a great big net!
We're in the air
and very wet!

We're coming down
on a great big boat—
the biggest
fishing boat afloat!

You got caught with our fish.
Sorry about that!
Excuse me, sir—
but that's one of ours
under your hat!

Pa, we still have
a fish to get!
We have not caught
our dinner yet!

No problem, son.
No need to fuss!
We'll buy our fish
from Grizzly Gus!

My best advice
to both of you
is to do what Mama
says to do!

Ah! A fish that's tender.
A fish that's sweet.
A fish that's good
for a bear to eat!